The Worldwide Adventures of Winston and Churchill

Book One
Europe

Written by
Michael Finklea

Illustrated by
Wesley Ortiz

Ozark Publishing • P.O. Box 79217 • Atlanta, Georgia 30357-2217 • 800-321-5671

Library of Congress cataloging-in-publication data

Finklea, Michael, 1962-

iv

The Worldwide Adventures of Winston and Churchill

Book One
Europe

To Nikki

<u>Dedicated to</u>
authors Dave and Pat Sargent for encouraging me to write
and especially for their love and support in making it possible!

<u>Special thanks to</u>
- William Conrad for giving me the idea of having my two characters travel the world and for choosing mice. I would have probably picked goats.
- David Sargent Jr. for the endless hours he endured with me reading to him over and over and over again.
- Chris Long for the huge amounts of encouragement and support over the years.
- Brian Garmon for helping me through the sections of information that you can't always find in books.
- For information on particular countries, author used data gathered from the 1997 CD-Rom Mac version of Grolier Multimedia Encyclopedia, Danbury, CT.

Introduction

"Churchill! Churchill! In the words of one of our famous distant cousins, Senior Speedy, . . . **Andale, Andale, Arriba!** We have exactly thirty minutes to make it to the airport and sneak onto our flight. I refuse to believe you have waited until the last minute to finish packing."

Like every other trip in the history of trips, Winston's and Churchill's was no exception. They were getting off to a late start.

"Churchill, did you pack your camera?"

"Uh-huh!"

"Did you pack your p.j.'s?"

"Yep!"

"Did you pack the snacks for the plane ride?"

"Oh yes! We have cheese toast, cheese fries, cheese balls, cheese sticks, cheese whiz, and now *say 'cheese,'* because we're off."

The camera flashed, and the first picture marked the beginning of *The Worldwide Adventures of Winston and Churchill.*

Not since Brookshire, the royal castle cat, had chased their family out of merry ole' England, have two little mice set sail on such a big adventure!

Chapter One

Bon Voyage!
(Good Trip!)

*Y*ou see, Winston and Churchill are brothers and direct descendants of the *Royal Rodent Family of England*.

After being chased out of merry ole' England by that fuzzy feline, the boys' parents moved them to America while they were still quite young and just nibbling on cream cheese.

Recently receiving notice that their two English cousins, Maggie and Thatcher, had joined the "Mice Capades," the boys decided to surprise them by flying to London, England, and attending their opening night.

So, with a little time on their hands, the two little mice decided that they would make this the trip of a lifetime. They would also travel to visit relatives all around the world!

For the last couple of weeks, Winston and Churchill have been carefully planning out the details for their big trip. They have decided to travel to the seven continents, visiting their distant relatives to learn a little bit more about the countries where they lived. Everyone had been contacted except their cousins Boris and Yeltsin in Russia. As luck would have it, they were on vacation too!

And, what better time to travel? For Winston has just graduated from the University of Wisconsin by correspondence. That meant he had taken his classes by mail and now had a degree in geography with a second degree in foreign languages.

Winston was very worldly and would be the perfect tour guide. He was obviously smart; in fact, he could speak seven different languages. Convenient, wouldn't you say, since they would be traveling to seven different continents!

He was charming, dashingly handsome, and, best of all, he was *already packed!*

Winston

Churchill

Winston could hardly wait to see all of the places he had been studying about for the past four years.

Churchill, on the other hand, had never ventured past the next-door deli of their upper eastside New York basement apartment. He was a bit naive. That just meant that he hadn't experienced as much as his older brother.

He was your typical young mouse next door, very inquisitive. But, he did know a lot about cheese. In fact, if they gave college degrees for cheese smarts, Churchill would have graduated number one in his class!

Churchill remembered very little about his short time in England, so he was eager to see what the world had to offer. He had his map, his camera, his passport, and a lot of questions just resting on the tip of his tongue.

"Churchill, are you ready to go yet?"

"Okay, yes, I'm ready. Now, remember, Winston, my legs are not as long as yours.

"Hey, Winston, how do they define what a continent is exactly?"

Winston pulled out his atlas and opened it to the section on Europe.

"Okay, Churchill, look at this map and I'll show you. A continent is considered a continuous area of landmass above and below sea level."

As Churchill studied the map, he noticed that England, also known as Great Britain, was not connected to Europe.

"Well then I'm confused, Winston. It doesn't look like England is part of Europe since it is not connected. There is water between the two lands. Why would this be considered the same continent?"

"That's a good question," Winston replied. "The land can be connected under the water. The area of water separating England from Europe is called the English Channel. An example here in the United States would be the Hawaiian islands or the island of Cuba. Even though Cuba is sixty miles off the coast of Florida, the land beneath the Gulf of Mexico connects the two sides."

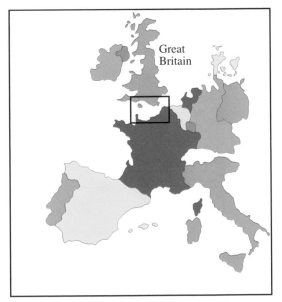

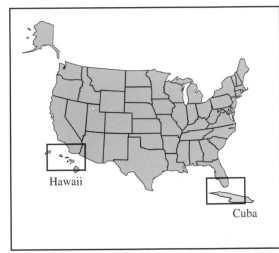

6

Australia

Antarctica

Europe

North America

Africa

South America

Asia

"Okay, what about Europe and Asia, Winston? They are connected. Why would they be considered two continents?"

"I'm very impressed, Churchill! You are right. Europe and Asia are connected, but they are treated as separate continents because of historical rather than geographic reasons.

"There are seven different continents around the world, Churchill. The continents, in order of size from the smallest to the largest, are Australia, Europe, Antarctica, Africa, North America, South America, and Asia.

"Did you know they say there are more than one hundred and seventy independent countries in the world? Some of the largest countries include Russia, Canada, China, the United States, and Australia. Australia is not only its own continent, but it's also its own country. Each of these countries has its own cultural identity.

"Europe will be our first stop!"

Chapter Two

Fasten Your Seat Belts!

uring the plane ride over, Churchill began preparing his famous assorted cheese tray as a gift to Maggie and Thatcher. He couldn't help but think about all of the things they had talked about earlier.

"You know, Winston, learning different facts about the world will be lots of fun and very interesting. In fact, I want to learn something about each of the continents that we will be visiting."

"Good, Churchill! That's the spirit! Did you know that Europe is the second smallest continent, and there are still over 788 million people that live there? In fact, there are thirty-eight different countries in Europe. Some of the countries include Austria, Belgium, Greece, Iceland, Poland, Portugal, Spain, and Switzerland.

"We will be traveling to England, France, Germany, Sweden, Russia, and Italy."

Churchill couldn't believe his own ears and almost choked on a peppered jack cheese wedge!

"So, Europe is the second smallest continent and still has that many people and countries included in it?"

"That's right, Churchill. And in all of those countries, Europe is the only continent that doesn't have deserts."

"Well, I'll be a mouse's uncle." Churchill exclaimed. "Do you know the language they speak?"

"Churchill, a mouse's uncle? I believe the saying is 'I'll be a monkey's uncle.' Anyway, there are many different languages spoken in Europe, but don't worry, in England they speak English."

"Sorry! You know my sayings are a little mixed up at times. Is London the largest city in Europe?"

"No. Moscow, Russia, is the largest city. Paris, France, is second. London, England, is the third largest," Winston explained.

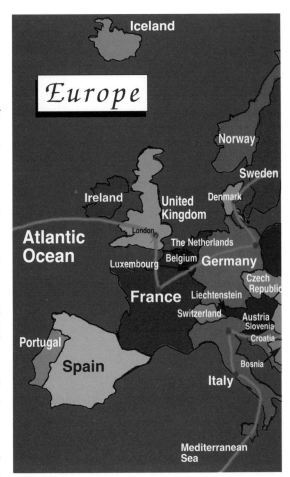

The boys talked for hours. Well, it was more like Churchill asked a lot of questions, and Winston answered them!

"Winston, am I asking you too many questions?"

"No. Don't ever think that, Churchill. You can never ask too many questions. The more questions you ask, the more you learn."

By now, the big, friendly blue sky had turned dark. For that matter, it had been dark for hours. They had spent most of the night talking about all of the things they wanted to see and do in Europe. But they knew they could do only a small number of them, since they could spend about a day in each country. So, by the time they were falling asleep, they both had decided that they would see each of the capital cities in each of the countries they had chosen to visit. If they had any extra time, they would also try and visit other areas as well.

London

The Pound

Chapter Three
England

England is the largest of the parts of the United Kingdom. It occupies the southern and southeastern part of the island of Great Britain and is bordered on the west by Wales and on the north by Scotland. More than forty-six million people live there. London is the capital of England.

$\mathcal{T}$he boys were suddenly awakened in the early morning hours by the voice of the captain telling everyone to buckle their seat belts, and, of course, put their tray tables and their seat backs in the upright positions!

As Churchill peeked out from under the seat, he whispered to Winston, "Are we there? Are we there yet?" He was so excited, he would just as soon have parachuted out of that plane than wait for it to land. "How long was the plane ride?"

Winston answered "Yes, we're here! It took us only five hours to fly from New York City to London." The two of them had crawled up the back of the seat and peeked out the window. "Wow, Churchill. We just flew over the Atlantic Ocean!"

After gathering their knapsacks, the boys hit the streets running and dodging in and out of big feet everywhere.

They would be spending most of the day by themselves, since cousins Maggie and Thatcher were still preparing for the Mice Capades' first show.

"Okay, Churchill, London is a big city with a lot of things to see. So, let's first locate Maggie and Thatcher's *flat*, and then let's sample some of the local cuisine. How would you like to try *bangers and mash*?"

"The *flat* and *bangers and mash*?" Churchill looked puzzled. "I thought you said they spoke English."

Winston explained that many words have different meanings in England than they have in the United States. For example, in England, gasoline is called petrol. Elevators are called lifts. Cookies are called biscuits. Apartments are called flats. And bangers and mash is made out of thick sausages with mashed potatoes.

May 9th. Our first day in London!
I was trying to show Winston how to be street smart.
If we walk with a purpose, they won't mess with us!

14

Well, lunch was unusual, but very tasty. Churchill noticed that people were not using the U.S. form of money when they paid the bill.

Winston explained, "The value of money in other countries is figured out using what they call the exchange rate. One of our U.S. dollars equals sixty-two cents in England."

Churchill looked at Winston like he was crazy. He decided that day that Winston would be responsible for paying for everything on the trip. He would just be responsible for having fun. Churchill wanted to learn as much as he could, but figuring out foreign currency was not one of them. Besides, he couldn't remember the last time they had to pay for anything, anyway. They were mice!

Winston laughed. "It does seem a little confusing at first, but don't worry, you'll get the hang of it."

Well, lunch was over, their little stomachs were full, and it was time to do some sightseeing. Churchill grabbed his camera, and they were off! They would travel around London on their subway system known as "the tube."

They both decided that since London was so large, they would visit only some of the places that they had heard most about.

In a city of seven million people being organized is important, so they ran up a leg of a nearby park bench and planned out their day. Because believe me, when you're only four inches tall, you need a plan before you take off on foot, anywhere.

"Okay, Churchill, are you ready, or would you like another spot of tea first?"

"No, thank you, Winston, my good chap. Talle ho."

The first stop, of course, would be Buckingham Palace to see the changing of the guard. This is the London home of the queen and the entire royal family. There are periods of time where part of the palace is open to the public. That didn't matter to Churchill. He was determined to visit all six hundred rooms! He figured that in a palace that large, there just had to be a mouse in that house! And, he just knew it would be another cousin.

Buckingham Palace

Next, they visited Big Ben, the famous bell for the British Houses of Parliament. The boys were really excited when they reached Parliament Square, where statues were located of statesmen from long ago. Among the statues were Abraham Lincoln and Winston Churchill!

The boys remembered their mother talking about the famous man that they had been named after. Winston Churchill led Britain through the most terrible and desperate time of its history. He helped in stopping Hitler's invasion into England.

Churchill saluting a horse and almost getting stepped on.

16

Maggie and Thatcher during their solo act.

The four of us laughing at Churchill's cheezy jokes.

While dressed up and on their way in to be seated at the show, Winston talked about England's rich history. William Shakespeare, who is considered the greatest writer of all time, and Sir Isaac Newton, one of history's most important scientists, were both born in England.

"Look, Winston. Don't make a squeak. Here they are." The boys' eyes looked like they were really ready to pop out of their heads—even more than usual. They were so proud. Maggie and Thatcher had the starring roles!

Needless to say, the Mice Capades was a smash! The boys went backstage to surprise Maggie and Thatcher with one of the most breathtaking, mouthwatering, eyecatching cheese tray displays that probably had ever been created. Churchill used cheddar and Stilton cheeses, both of which originally came from England.

The four of them spent the rest of the night catching up and talking about old times. They promised that even though they couldn't stay to visit, they would return again soon.

The Franc

Chapter Four
France

France is an independent nation in Western Europe. It is the largest Western European country. France is shaped roughly like a hexagon, and three of its six sides are bounded by water—the English Channel on the northwest, the Atlantic Ocean and Bay of Biscay on the west, and the Mediterranean Sea on the southeast. The remaining sides are shared by seven European neighbors—Belgium and Luxembourg on the northeast; Germany, Switzerland, and Italy on the east; and Spain and tiny Andorra on the south. France's eighth neighbor is Monaco, located on the Mediterranean coast near Nice.

Paris is the capital of France.

*I*t was hard for Churchill to believe they were in an entirely different country, and it only took a thirty-minute plane ride to get from London to Paris, France!

They were thrilled when they exited the plane, for waiting to greet them were their French cousins, Marie and Antoinette.

Antoinette threw out her arms and with a huge smile said, "Bonjour, Monsieur Winston and Monsieur Churchill. Comma talle vous?"

Churchill looked at Winston and said, "What do you think she meant by that?"

As Winston hugged his distant cousins and kissed them once on each side of their cheek, as a customary greeting, he answered, "Churchill, she was not talking about you. 'Monsieur' simply means mister, and 'comma talle vous' means how are you?"

Marie and Antoinette whisked them off to their beautiful penthouse apartment on the top floor of the Eiffel Tower. The view from this sky-high corner room was 984 feet off the ground. Now that's a view!

Marie explained that the Eiffel Tower was built for the Paris Exposition of 1889. It is one of Paris's most famous sights.

Later that afternoon, they visited the famous, beautiful cathedral of Notre Dame. The cathedral was dedicated to the Virgin Mary and was built between 1163 and the year 1200. As Churchill looked up with his mouth wide open, Marie explained that the building was damaged during the French Revolution but had been restored during the last century.

Eiffel Tower

Churchill learned that the French form of currency was "the franc," but he wasn't ready to master working with the exchange rate. He kept telling Winston that it would be so much easier if it were all the same.

They traveled by subway here in Paris, also. Their subway was called "the metro."

Notre Dame

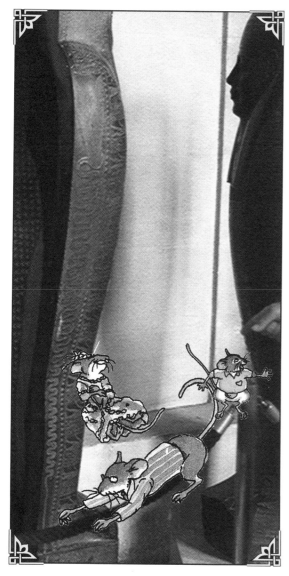

Marie stated that Paris is a small city for being a capital of a country. It is more than two thousand years old and was conquered by Julius Caesar in 52 B.C.

On the second day, they went to the Palace of Versailles. It was the beautiful home for each of the French kings during the time they ruled. Marie and Antoinette were named after the queen of the last French king, Louis XVI.

Winston whispered, "XVI are the Roman numerals for the sixteenth. See, Marie Antoinette led up the French Revolution. She was not liked by her countrymen and was famous for treating them badly. She ended up being executed by guillotine for treason. In other words, they chopped her head off!"

Just as Winston had finished his statement, Marie happened to take a picture of Churchill almost getting knocked off the pole. Winston felt bad for him, but he was more upset that it wasn't caught on video. He just knew he'd have had that $10,000 prize in the bag!

On the morning of the third day, they had decided to spend one extra day traveling with their cousins through France to the southeastern city of Nice (Neice) near the border of Italy, where they would part ways. They knew this would put them one day behind schedule, but they really wanted to see the countryside.

"Antoinette, how far are we from Italy?" quizzed Churchill.

"Italy is fifteen miles to the east!"

Churchill still couldn't believe how close everything seemed.

Antoinette continued. "And about one hundred miles west is the city of Marseille (mahr-say'). It is the main sea port, and the second most populated city in France. It was founded over two thousand five hundred years ago! Marseille is the most important port on the Mediterranean Sea. Major imports include wines, fruits, and animal skins."

"Animal skins! Okay, it's time to change the subject again." This fact made Churchill a little too nervous.

A day of beauty spent at a water fall in Nice, France.

Churchill determined to take a cheese souvenir back with him. Of course, he wouldn't listen to me and take the french fry.

They were all having such a good time, but it was getting dark now and it was time to say good-bye. The boys thanked their cousins again and again for being such wonderful tour guides.

Churchill started to drag away his only souvenir: a five-pound block of Roquefort cheese! This crumbly, streaked, blue cheese is made from sheep's milk, and originated in France.

He, also, finally had a chance to sample some of the famous French cuisine he had heard so much about. Of course, Churchill didn't see what all of the fuss was about. He had eaten french fries many times before, but it was kind of exciting to be able to sample what he considered the real thing!

Later that night as they were drifting off to sleep, Churchill turned and looked at Winston and said, "Thank you, 'Monsieur' Winston, for bringing me. 'Comma talle vous?'"

Winston smiled and replied, "That's very good, Churchill. I'm fine, just fine."

 Berlin

The Mark

Chapter Five
Germany

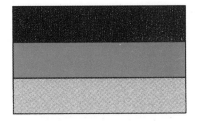

Germany, a unified country from 1871 to 1945, was divided after World War II into two states: the Federal Republic of Germany (West Germany) and the German Democratic Republic (East Germany). In 1990, following the collapse of communism, East Germany voted for unification of the two sides.

Located in Central Europe, unified Germany is bordered on the north by the North Sea, Denmark, and the Baltic Sea; on the east by Poland and the Czech Republic; on the south by Austria and Switzerland; and on the west by France, Luxembourg, Belgium, and the Netherlands.

Berlin is the capital of Germany.

kay, Churchill. We are now entering the central part of Europe."

"I've always wanted to visit Germany, Winston. Do we have any relatives here that we will be meeting?"

"Yes, and here they are now. Churchill, I would like to introduce you to your cousin Auto and your cousin Bonnie, the two fastest mice in all of Germany. And, as if things have not been moving fast enough, you might want to tighten your shoelaces because the world-wide adventures are about to turn into the whirlwind adventures!"

"Well, I thought . . ."

Before Churchill could finish his statement, Auto and Bonnie were halfway down the street. All they could hear was Bonnie's faint voice saying, "Hurry, come this way, we'll take the train."

25

Once they boarded the train, Auto told the boys that Germany has Europe's most modern and extensive transportation system and high-speed superhighways, like that little old highway they had been named after, the Autobahn. The Autobahn has no speed limits!

"Did you catch that, Winston? Auto and Bonnie—the Autobahn. I just figured it out. You have to get up pretty early to fool me. The early bird picks up germs. Right, Winston?"

"What did you say, Churchill? I believe you meant, 'the early bird catches the worm.' I think that's what you are trying to say. Isn't it?"

Churchill smiled and continued. "Is Berlin the capital of Germany, and do you know of any place that we can get our little paws on some sauerkraut?"

"Berlin is the capital," answered Auto. "And we'll find sauerkraut on the dining car. Is sauerkraut is your favorite food?"

"Yuk! No, we just want to try a new dish from each country we will be visiting. I thought this would be a good time to try it."

My mission is clear. I have to get Winston to relax. He finally unbuttoned his jacket in Germany!

The view from the top of the Gothic Cathedral.

As they traveled north, they passed through many of Germany's cities. They had managed to find an empty compartment on the train, so the four mice sat on the windowsill and had the entire day to visit with one another.

Winston and Churchill were beginning to realize that it did not matter which country they were in or what language their cousins spoke, that mice, like people, were really the same, and they all had things in common!

The first city they passed through was Munich (mue'-nik), the original capital and principal city of Germany. Munich is located near the Austrian border and is only about thirty miles north of the Alps. The city's name means "home of the monks."

In the city of Cologne (Koln), the train finally stopped and they all four jumped off and followed a tour group through the German countryside to one of Cologne's famous sights, the Gothic Cathedral. It has really tall twin five-hundred-and-fifteen-foot towers and beautiful stained-glass windows.

27

Along the west side of Germany, they passed through the city of Dusseldorf. Bonnie explained that it is now among the leading German manufacturing centers of women's clothing and cosmetics. She wished that they had enough time to find an outlet mall, but she didn't want to take a chance and miss the train.

For dinner, they were thrilled to eat in the train's dining car. And, with Winston's help, Churchill pretended to pay the bill with Germany's form of currency, the deutsche mark (doych mark). He had no idea how much he was supposed to hand over to Winston, nor did he care. He was too delighted with his grilled German Muenster cheese sandwich!

The next day, they all four spent the day in Berlin with half of the day alone spent at the famous Berlin Wall, the hated symbol of the divided city. A few sections of the wall still remain standing and are used as art galleries.

Bonnie gave the boys a quick history lesson. "Did you know that Germany and Berlin used to be divided in half? The two

Now this is living. Oh, yes. Life if good. And tasty, too!

sides were separated by what was known as the Berlin Wall. Since 1990 and the fall of communism, Germany is a free and united country. In fact, store windows still have maps of East and West Germany with band-aids connecting them. This was a symbol of the unification of the two sides of the country."

"How interesting. Band-aids, huh? So, they used band-aids because you would use a band-aid to help mend a hurt or a cut, right? And they used them as a symbol of helping mend the two countries separation."

"Touché, Churchill. I don't think I could have explained it any better myself!" Winston couldn't help but notice that Churchill's eyes were glued to Bonnie. He could see how exciting this trip was going to be. He knew that Churchill loved the idea of learning something about each of the places.

At the end of the day, Auto and Bonnie invited the boys to spend the night at their place, so they could get a good night sleep before taking off for Sweden.

Things were happening awfully fast for the two little mice, but they never lost their excitement. They knew they would have to keep a fast pace, and they figured they could rest when they got back home. As in most trips, Winston and Churchill were going to need a vacation after their vacation.

The next morning, as they were walking out the door, Churchill saw a short note that Winston had left for their two cousins. The note thanked them for all of their wonderful German hospitality and ended with two foreign words *"danke schöen!"*

Winston explained to Churchill that *"danke schöen"* means "thank you" in German!

Stockholm

The Krone

Chapter Six

Sweden

Sweden is the largest of the five Nordic countries and forms part of Scandinavia in northwestern Europe. Sweden shares a long land frontier with Norway to the west. Finland, and the Baltic Sea are to the east, and Denmark lies to the south. The Baltic Sea islands are integral parts of Sweden.

Stockholm is the capital of Sweden.

$\mathcal{F}$rom Germany, the boys sailed a short distance across the Baltic Sea to Copenhagen, Denmark's capital city.

Winston explained, "Of the five Nordic nations, Denmark is the smallest and Sweden is the largest. Sweden is where we will meet up with cousins Bianca and Borgiheimer."

Once in Copenhagen, they hopped a plane to Sweden and hurried to meet their two Swedish cousins in Stockholm, the capital and largest city.

As the boys entered Stockholm, their cousins were right where they said they would be, playing tennis on the first tennis court as you enter the city on the right.

"Hi! I'm Winston and this is Churchill. You must be Bianca and Borgiheimer."

"Yes. It's nice to meet you. But just call us Bjon (Bion) and Borg for short."

31

Bjon asked if they would like to get to know each another over a tennis set, but poor Winston and Churchill never stood a chance. After losing three games in a row, the boys quickly diverted their attention to sightseeing.

As the four of them scurried into the downtown area of Stockholm, Winston was surprised to hear that the city was spread out over fourteen islands.

"Will you be able to visit the Arctic Circle? It is in the northern part of Sweden," said Bjon.

Winston answered, "No, we will not have time this trip, but I have heard that it is very beautiful. We were going to leave for Russia tonight."

As Bjon took off her mini warm-up jacket, she remarked, "At least you caught us at a good time of the year. Even though we are furry, it can get pretty chilly up here during the winter. I used to live in Alta. That's in the Arctic Circle.

"You realize, depending on which way the earth is tilting, and because parts of Sweden are so far north, the summers can have twenty-four hours of sunlight. The winters, on the other hand, can have twenty-four hours a day of darkness!"

Winston, of course, knew this, but Churchill was, once again, shocked. Why was he always to receive such shocking news while taking a bite of cheese? This time he almost choked on a piece of swiss!

"Excuse me for interrupting, Bjon. Churchill, why are you eating swiss cheese? You know that swiss cheese is not from Sweden. It's from Switzerland."

"Of course I realize that. Who here is the cheese expert anyway? It's just that I don't know of a cheese from Sweden. But, since swiss starts with an 's' and I am hungry, I thought swiss cheese was the next best thing!"

One of our favorite local restaurants.
Winston had three servings of spaghetti and swedish meatballs.

Let's see . . . what was going through my head? Oh, yes,
I remember. "HEY Winston! How about giving me a hand!?"

They all agreed with Churchill's logic. So, with cheese in hand, they ventured on.

It was surprising to see how much of the architecture around the area was new and modern. Bjon told them that they had to find new and alternate ways to build because of the limited availability of the land necessary to produce materials for construction.

Borg asked, "Can you stay one extra day? We could take you on in another game of tennis. Both of you against one of us?"

"No, but thanks. We know that you are named after the famous Swedish tennis player Bjon Borg. No, we must press on. Winston has given me a precise itinerary to follow."

"Well then, you should take that night ferry across the Baltic Sea to Finland. Finland borders Russia. If you catch a train there, you will be in Russia by morning."

As the ferry was pulling away, they had to say their quick good-byes! They just barely made it. A good thing, too, with those little short legs, they couldn't have jumped far.

Moscow

The Ruble

Chapter Seven

Russia

Russia is the largest country in the world, extending from the Baltic Sea in the west to the Pacific Ocean in the east, and occupying more than half of the Eurasian landmass. Russia is bounded on the west by Norway, Finland, Estonia, Latvia, Belarus, and Ukraine; on the south by the Black Sea, Georgia, Azerbaijan, Kazakhstan, Mongolia, and China; on the east by the Pacific Ocean; and on the north by the Arctic Ocean. The area west of the Ural Mountains is called European Russia; the Asian part of the country, east of the Urals, is called Siberia. Only European Russia is shown above.

Moscow is the capital of Russia.

*A*s they exited the train in the city of Saint Petersburg, Churchill was reminded that Russia was one of the countries where they would not have tour guides. Since cousins Boris and Yeltsin were also on vacation, they were on their own!

They had spent a lot of time on foreign lands lately, but never alone. Russian was one language in which Winston could not even say "hello" much less ask for directions.

Of course, this did not slow down Churchill. Before Winston could stand back up after picking up their knapsacks and the roquefort cheese, Churchill was already posing in front of the famous statue of Peter the Great. He read on a sign that Peter was the founder of Saint Petersburg and was Russia's first emperor.

After walking around for a while, they spotted a vacation guide that had not quite made it into a trash can. They decided that they would sneak aboard a tour boat floating down the Volga River through the Russian countryside to Moscow, Russia's capital city, and just spend the day there.

"Hey, Winston, the article in this guide says that Russia used to headquarter the world communist movement. But, it says that in December 1991, after the Soviet Union was dissolved, Russia was reborn as an independent country."

"Yes, Churchill. That is why there is no longer the *Berlin Wall* separating East and West Germany. You know, it is too bad that we couldn't locate Boris and Yeltsin. They were named after Russia's current president. Boris Yeltsin was the major force behind the formation of the Independent States in 1991 and the breakup of the USSR.

"Churchill, since Russia is so large, and since we don't have any tour guides, let's wait until we get to the continent of Asia to visit more of the eastern side of the country. Okay? Did you realize that half of Russia is in Europe, and the other half is in Asia?"

"Sure. Whatever." Churchill was too busy running back and forth trying to jump onto the boat.

If there was one thing you could say about Churchill, he could never get his sayings straight, but he was easy to please! Well that, and that he knew every type of cheese ever made. As he looked at his map, he saw that Russia stretched from the Ukraine all the way around the world to Alaska and the Pacific Ocean! The two sides of the country were separated by the Ural Mountains.

The Kremlin.

Once on board, they listened to the tour guide talk about how Saint Petersburg spans over more than one hundred islands! The city is connected by over six hundred and thirty-five bridges. In the northern location, they have "white nights." As they learned in Sweden, they also experience twenty-four hours of daylight in June and July.

Later, the guide started talking about Moscow and how the city had developed over the years as a series of circles. Each one of the new circles encompassed the previous one. The center of this series of circles is the Kremlin. The Kremlin is Russia's most famous walled fortress. Inside the walls are some of Russia's most spectacular churches and museums.

They knew they would be able to visit Russia once they arrived in Asia. So, they spent some of the day at the Kremlin, and the rest of the day running around the streets through the circular formations like they were running around on an exercise wheel.

Rome

The Lira

Chapter Eight
Italy

Italy is an independent nation in southern Europe. It extends southward from the Alps to the Mediterranean Sea, forming a narrow, boot-shaped peninsula reaching almost to the northern coast of Africa. It is advantageously located to control traffic between the eastern and western basins of the Mediterranean. Italy is bordered on the northwest by France, on the north by Switzerland, on the northeast by Austria, and on the east by Yugoslavia.

Rome is the capital of Italy.

*A*fter flying from Moscow over the countries of the Ukraine, Hungary, and Bosnia, the boys landed in Milan, Italy. They had just one thing on their minds. Where was the best place to find an authentic, extra-large, cheese pizza pie? Churchill wanted this pizza made with all of the Italian cheeses: mozzarella, provolone, ricotta, with Parmesan sprinkled on top! The only cheese he would be leaving off would be cottage cheese, which also originates from Italy!

"Come on, Churchill, we'll find a pizza as we stroll through Milan."

As Winston looked down at the map he commented, "Churchill, I don't know if I've ever told you about my big dream. My dream is to have legs at least four feet longer and walk down a '*cat walk*' in an Italian fashion show."

"A *cat-walk*? That sounds frightening!" Churchill was having a very difficult time imagining this.

Winston explained how some of the most important trends in fashion are created here by some of the world's leading designers. Winston's dream was to live on the edge of fashion.

"Churchill, after we leave Milan, we will be meeting up with cousins Michel and Angelo in Rome. We are supposed to meet them tomorrow night at a local coffeehouse. I hear they are more of the 'artsy' type."

Later that day they headed for Rome, Italy's capital and its largest city.

Once they arrived in Rome, they located the coffeehouse. But how were they going to be sure who their cousins were?

Churchill looked over in the corner at two possible candidates. "Are you, by chance, Michel and Angelo?"

"Why, yes, yes, we are!" answered Michel.

A cat walk, huh? I don't think so. That's not a dream. That's a nightmare!

I think I take after the hip mice in the family. Winston takes more after Dad.

Oops! I accidentally took home Michel's skiing picture. It's a good thing they didn't hit a brush pile on those match sticks!

They spoke Italian most of night . . . I wish Angelo would have handed me that paint brush. I'd have show him a thing or two.

Winston looked surprised. "You speak English?"

"Well, actually, I speak English. Angelo only speaks Italian."

As the four sat under the table, Angelo painted a small portrait of the view outside as seen through a crack in the wall. Michel showed the boys a snapshot of himself and Angelo as they returned from skiing in the Alps.

"Oh, how exciting. Isn't that somewhere in Colorado?" asked Churchill.

"No, not exactly," answered Michel. "The Alps are just above the northern border of Italy."

Michel pointed to Italy on Churchill's map. "See, Italy starts just below the Alps and continues down to the Mediterranean Sea, forming a narrow, boot-shaped peninsula. It almost reaches the northern coast of Africa."

"Yes, we know. That is why we ended our tour through Europe in Italy. It should only take us an hour to cross the Mediterranean Sea."

"Well, welcome to Italy. We are so glad you had a chance to visit us. We just love it here in Rome. Look outside. Isn't is beautiful? That river that you are looking at, Churchill, is the Tiber River." Michel could tell that Churchill was excited. "The Tiber flows through Rome from north to south, dividing the city. On the east bank is the most visible and plentiful remains of classical Rome.

"To the northwest and along the Tiber is more of medieval Rome. That's where the many squares, fountains, statues, and palaces were built for which Rome is famous. On the west bank of the Tiber River is Vatican City. It is the central government of the Roman Catholic Church and the home of its spiritual leader, the Pope."

"*How long will you be in town?*" asked Angelo in Italian.

Winston answered in Italian, "Tonight only."

"Yes, unfortunately we won't be able to visit long. Later tonight, we will need to start toward Sicily and then go on to Africa."

"Oh, how exciting. Will you be doing any hunting?" asked Michel.

Winston answered, "No, I just hope that *we* are not hunted."

As the boys said good-bye, Angelo handed them his painting as a souvenir for their visit. And Churchill finally learned a little more about the famous painter for which his cousins were named. The famous Italian Michelangelo was perhaps the greatest artist of western civilization. He created wonderful works of painting, sculpture, and architecture. He was noted for the beautiful painting on the ceiling of the Sistine Chapel, depicting the creation of man. The immense project he undertook took four years to complete.

The ceiling of the Sistine Chapel.

What a delightful treat to see. What a wonderful gift to end their last night in Europe.

That night, the boys traveled by gondola to Sicily, where they would depart for Africa. Churchill stopped and turned to the north to wave good-bye to all of his European cousins. He then turned back toward the south, walked to the edge of the water, and as he looked across in the direction in which they were headed, yelled, **"AFRICA, HERE WE COME!"**

List of countries in Europe

Albania	Germany	Netherlands
Austria	Greece	Norway
Belarus	Hungary	Poland
Belgium	Iceland	Portugal
Bosnia	Ireland	Rumania
Bulgaria	Italy	Russia
Croatia	Latvia	Slovakia
Czech Republic	Liechtenstein	Slovenia
Denmark	Lithuania	Spain
Estonia	Luxembourg	Sweden
Finland	Macedonia	Switzerland
France	Moldova	Turkey
	Montenegro	United Kingdom